First published in the UK by HarperCollins Children's Books in 2009
1 3 5 7 9 10 8 6 4 2
ISBN: 978-0-00-730160-7
A CIP catalogue record for this title is available from the British Library.

Printed and bound in China

NODDY

Noddy and the Magic Rubber

by Enid Blyton

Contents

1.   Bert Monkey Comes to Noddy
2.   Bert Monkey Tells His Tale
3.   Off to Skittle Town
4.   In Toy-Cat Village
5.   A Reward for the Rubber
6.   Noah's Ark Town
7.   What a Peculiar Thing!
8.   Back to Toy Town
9.   Master Tubby Bear Has a Good Time
10. Little Tubby is Very Naughty
11. Noddy Gets the Rubber at Last
12. The End of the Adventure

BERT MONKEY CYCLED UP TO NODDY'S
LITTLE FRONT DOOR ·

—⊸ 1 ⊷—

BERT MONKEY COMES TO NODDY

LITTLE Noddy was just finishing his breakfast one fine morning when he heard somebody ringing a bicycle bell very loudly indeed.

"Oh – that's Big-Ears! He's come to see me!" He looked out of the window – but it wasn't Big-Ears. It was somebody else.

"It's that silly Bert Monkey!" said Noddy. "I hope he isn't coming here."

Bert Monkey came cycling to Noddy's little front door, ringing his bell and whistling loudly.

He was dressed in red shorts, a blue coat and a funny round hat. He had a bow at the end of his tail. Noddy thought that he looked very silly.

"Rat-a-tatta-tat, RAT-TAT!" That was Bert Monkey knocking at Noddy's door.

"There's no need to break my door down!" said Noddy crossly, opening the door. "What's all the noise about?"

"Oh, Noddy I want your help," said Bert Monkey, and he put his tail through Noddy's arm.

"Don't," said Noddy, and pushed the tail away.

"How do you want my help?"

"Can I come in and tell you?" said Bert Monkey. "I don't want everyone to hear."

"Whatever is it?" said Noddy. "You can come in if you make your tail behave itself. Last time you came to see me your tail knocked a cup and saucer off my table."

"I'll put it in my pocket," said Bert, and he stuffed his tail into his shorts pocket. It came out at once and he stuffed it in again, bow and all.

"I'm glad I haven't a tail like yours," said Noddy. "Always into mischief – look, it's out again. *Don't* let it take my teapot lid off, Bert!"

Bert Monkey stuffed his tail into his pocket again, but it came out quickly and waved itself under Noddy's nose. Noddy pushed it away.

"For goodness sake, sit down on your tail," he said to Bert Monkey. "And please sit down hard."

"That's a good idea," said Bert, and he sat down hard on his tail. "Now listen, Noddy, I'm in trouble."

"That's nothing new," said little Noddy. "You're always in trouble – you and that tail of yours."

"Yes, but this is *bad* trouble," said Bert. "And it's all because of my tail, too."

"Well, tell me," said Noddy, pouring himself out another cup of tea.

So Bert began his tale – and a very queer one it was!

BERT MONKEY TELLS HIS TALE

"YESTERDAY, I went to see my old Grandma," said Bert monkey. "Well, she likes me – and she gave me a pencil box."

"That was nice of her," said Noddy. "Though I really can't think why she likes you."

"I looked into the pencil box," said Bert, "and it hadn't got a rubber. So I said. 'Oh dear – no rubber! Plenty of pencils and pens, and even a paint brush – but no rubber!'"

"And did your Grandma give you one?" said Noddy.

"No – but my tail got me one!" said Bert.

"Your *tail!* Whatever do you mean?" said Noddy, surprised. "Look it's come out from under you, Bert. Quick, put it back; it's tickling my legs."

"Get back, tail," said Bert, sternly. "Well, Noddy – somehow or other my tail found a nice big rubber at my Grandma's – and put it into my pocket."

"Bert – you *made* your tail get that rubber!" said Noddy. "You're a thief!"

Bert's tail slipped out from under him in a trice and struck Noddy hard on the hand.

"Don't!" said Noddy in alarm, and picked up a fork. "Just try and do that again, tail, and see what happens to you!"

"Put that fork down," said Bert. "You shouldn't call my tail a thief. Do listen, Noddy, and let me tell you the rest of my story."

"Well, go on," said Noddy, but he didn't put the fork down.

"Well, my Grandma found out that the rubber had gone, and now she wants me to bring it back," said Bert. "Because, you see, it's a very magic one."

"How is it magic?" said Noddy, spreading some jam on his toast.

"It rubs out anything," said Bert. "It doesn't just rub out mistakes in a book – it rubs out anything. I mean – if you rubbed your carpet with it it would at once make a hole in it. If you rubbed your teapot it would disappear."

"Good gracious!" said Noddy. "What a dangerous rubber! Well – why don't you take it back to your Grandma?"

"Because I haven't got it," said Bert.

"Haven't got it?" said Noddy.

"I SOLD HIM THE PENCIL BOX AND THE RUBBER TOO,"
SAID BERT

"No," Bert went on. "You see, on my way home I met Sam Skittle, and I sold him the pencil box, and the rubber too, for a shilling. I didn't really want the pencil box."

"I see. So you want me to take you to Skittle Town and get it back from Sam for you," said Noddy.

"Yes, please, Noddy – before Sam finds out the rubber is magic and begins to rub out all kinds of things," Bert said. "PLEASE do take me. It's too far for me to bicycle. I'll pay you well – look!"

He took out a purse and emptied it on to Noddy's little table. Goodness, what a lot of money!

"I don't think I *want* to take you," said Noddy.

"Why not?" asked Bert.

"That tail of yours would be such a bother in my car," said Noddy. "It would hoot the hooter and make a nuisance of itself."

"I'll keep my tail in my pocket, I promise I will," said Bert. "Noddy, please do take me to get that rubber. My Grandma will be so angry if I don't take it back. Please, Noddy. PLEASE!"

"Oh, all right," said Noddy, getting up. "Come along, we'll get the car."

OFF TO SKITTLE TOWN

IT wasn't very long before Noddy and Bert Monkey were in the little car, driving merrily along the road to Skittle Town.

"Parp-parp!" said the car to old Mrs Wobbly crossing the road. And "Parp-parp!" it said to Miss Little-Doll with her shopping basket.

Then it said "Parp-parp!" very loudly to nothing at all and it kept saying it. Noddy was surprised.

"What's the matter, little car?" he said. And then he frowned. "Bert Monkey, it's that tail of yours! It's hooting the hooter – and look, now it's trying to take the steering wheel and steer. WILL you look after it?"

They came to a sign-post that said, "To Skittle Town" and very soon they were there. The road was full of skittles doing their shopping. Noddy didn't bother to hoot at them, because they never minded being knocked down.

"That's the best thing about skittles," said Noddy, knocking over a small boy-skittle. "They simply love falling over. Now where does this friend of yours live?"

"Over there – look!" said Bert, pointing to a little crooked house. His tail came out of his pocket and pointed too. Then it poked

Noddy in the eye and put itself back into Bert's pocket.

"If I catch hold of that tail of yours I'll pull it off!" said Noddy fiercely. "Poking me in the eye like that!"

The car stopped at the little crooked house. A boy-skittle came to the gate and hailed Bert Monkey.

"Hallo, Bert! How's your tail?"

"The tail pulled itself out of Bert's pocket and solemnly shook hands with the skittle. Noddy really couldn't help laughing. What a terrible tail!

"Sam," said Bert, "I want that pencil box back that I gave you. I'll pay you back the money you gave me. Will you get it?"

"Right," said Sam Skittle and went into the house. He came out with the pencil box and gave it to Bert, who paid him a shilling.

"Thanks," he said, and was just putting it down beside him on the seat when his tail began to tap him on the shoulder. Tap-tap!

"What's your tail doing that for?" said Noddy, surprised. "Is it trying to tell you something?"

"Yes," said Bert. "What is it now, tail? Oh, you want me to open the pencil box? Right."

So he opened the box – and then he gave a cry. "The rubber isn't here! It's gone. Hey, Sam! Sam Skittle - where's the rubber? There was a nice big one in the box."

"Oh yes. I forgot about that," said Sam. "I've plenty of rubbers, so I gave it to little Miss Harriet Kitten. She lives in Toy-Cat Village a bit further on."

Bert Monkey gave a groan.

"Oh, bother, bother, bother!" he cried. "Noddy, will you drive me to Toy-Cat Village, please?"

"It's rather a long way," began Noddy, but Bert looked so miserable that he nodded his head fast. "All right, all right. I'll take you. I know you'll be in terrible trouble if you don't bring that rubber back!"

So away they went to Toy-Cat Village, and Bert's tail made itself a nuisance again, hooting at everyone they passed. It really was a most annoying tail.

—•◦ 4 ◦•—

IN TOY-CAT VILLAGE

NODDY soon saw when they were getting near to Toy-Cat Village, because all kinds of toy cats were about.

Some were riding bicycles, some walking, and one dear little kitten-cat was running along bowling a hoop. She wore a pink bonnet, and had most beautiful whiskers.

"Look – that's Miss Harriet Kitten!" said Bert Monkey. "What a bit of luck to meet her like this. Hey, Miss Kitten! Hey!"

"*Don't* shout at her like that," said Noddy. "Get out of the car politely and take off your hat to her."

So Bert Monkey got out of the car and went over to Miss Harriet Kitten. He took off his hat and bowed most politely. His tail slid round in front of him and tried to shake hands with Miss Kitten.

"Miss Kitten, I believe?" said Bert Monkey, trying to be as polite as he could, and pushing his tail to the back of him.

Miss Kitten held on to her hoop and looked at him out of her big kitten-eyes. She really was a dear little thing. Noddy wished he could take her to Big-Ears' house and let her make friends with Big-Ears' big black cat.

"What do you want?" said Miss Kitten.

"I want the rubber that Sam Skittle gave you," said Bert Monkey. "I'm so very sorry, but it happens to belong to my Grandma."

"But Sam *gave* it to me," said Harriet Kitten. "I want it myself. You shan't have it."

MISS KITTEN ENJOYED THE RIDE ROUND
TOY-CAT VILLAGE

Bert Monkey thought that Miss Kitten wasn't as nice as she looked. "Oh, please, Miss Kitten!" he said. "I really must have it back. I'll give you an ice cream if you'll let me have it."

"No," said Miss Kitten. "And take your nasty tail away. It's trying to get my hoop-stick."

Whatever was Bert to do? Noddy called to

him, "I'll give her a LOVELY ride in my car if she'll let you have the rubber."

"Ooooh!" said Miss Kitten in delight and gave Noddy a most beautiful smile. Even her whiskers smiled. Noddy smiled back and made room for her beside him. "You can go in the back," he told Bert, "and sit down HARD on your tail!"

Miss Kitten enjoyed the drive round Toy-Cat Village, and waved so much that Noddy's hat was almost knocked off a dozen times. His bell jingled happily and his head nodded. He didn't mind when her whiskers tickled his ear.

Bert frowned. He didn't like sitting at the back, holding the hoop and hoop-stick. He felt silly. He was glad when the ride came to an end. "Now what about that rubber?" Bert said to Miss Kitten when she got out.

"The rubber? Oh yes," said Harriet Kitten, and she put her hand into her pocket. "Oh dear – it's not here. It's rubbed a hole in my pocket and it must have fallen out! I'm so sorry!"

She went off, bowling her hoop, looking pretty as a picture. Oh dear – *now* what was Bert Monkey to do?

—◦❧ 5 ❧◦—

A REWARD FOR THE RUBBER

"I DON'T believe her, do you?" Bert said to Noddy. "She just wanted a ride for nothing!"

"Oh no – she was telling the truth, I'm sure," said Noddy, shocked. "You said that rubber rubbed out anything – well, it probably rubbed against the bottom of her pocket as she ran along – and rubbed out the stitches. Then it fell out. Goodness knows who picked it up!"

"What am I going to DO?" wailed Bert. "I can't go home without it! Noddy, do help me. Think of something."

Noddy sat and thought hard, his head nodding. Then his bell jingled very loudly. It always did when he had a good idea.

"I know! We'll write out a big notice and put it on the wall over there, offering a reward for whoever brings us your rubber."

"You really have got a lot of brains, Noddy," said Bert, and Noddy felt pleased.

They wrote out the notice together and put it up on the wall. It said:

LOST. A BIG OLD RUBBER.
TWO ICE CREAMS WILL BE GIVEN TO
ANYONE BRINGING IT TO BERT MONKEY
AT MR TOY-CAT'S SHOP TODAY.

"Now we'll go to Mr Toy-Cat's shop and have something to eat," said Bert Monkey. "We'll wait and see if anyone comes with the rubber. Oh, I DO hope someone comes."

They went to the shop, which had plenty of little tables where people were having lunch. Bert and Noddy sat down next to a table where a family of toy cats were tucking in to sardines and cream.

Noddy thought he would have tomato sandwiches, macaroons and ice cream, and Bert Monkey had a monkey-nut stew and fruit salad.

"Look at your tail!" said Noddy, eating his sandwiches. "It's playing with that boy-cat's tail. They will trip up the waitress soon. There

CRASH! THE CAT-WAITRESS FELL OVER
THEIR TAILS

now – they've tied themselves together. Can't you POSSIBLY look after your tail for a few minutes, Bert?"

CRASH!

The cat-waitress fell over the tied-together tails, and Bert got a big ice cream over his head and down his neck. What a to-do there was!

"I told you that would happen," said Noddy fiercely, and he pulled the two tails undone. Then he wiped the ice cream from Bert's head. Why had he ever come out with Bert Monkey? Look at everyone staring at them!

NOAH'S ARK TOWN

SOMEONE came up to their table. It was a very plump toy cat, wearing a top-hat and long trousers.

"Are you the ones who put up that notice?" he said.

"Yes," said Bert. "Have you found the rubber?"

"No, but my friend found it in the road," said Mr Toy-Cat. "He came over from Noah's Ark Town this morning, and I was just seeing him off at the bus stop when he saw the rubber and picked it up to give to one of his sons, Shem, Ham or Japheth."

"Oh, good!" said Bert. "What is his name, please, and where does he live in Noah's Ark Town?"

"He's one of the Mr Noahs there," said Mr Toy-Cat. "Ask for Mr Nat Noah – everyone knows him."

"Thank you," said Bert, pleased. "Come on, Noddy – off to Noah's Ark Town now. My word, we are getting about this morning, aren't we?"

"We certainly are," said Noddy. "Well, I hope we find your rubber this time, Bert Monkey, I really do."

Off they went again. It was quite a long way to Noah's Ark Town, but at last they got there. Goodness, what a lot of Noah's Arks everywhere! Some were little, some big, some had doors shut, and some hadn't.

The ones that were open had animals walking in and out in pairs.

"Now we must ask for Mr Nat Noah," said Noddy, looking all around. "Dear me, I'm glad we know his name. We would never be able to find him if we didn't, because all the Mr Noahs look exactly alike."

They certainly did. Six of them were standing talking together at a corner, all as like as peas in a pod. Noddy hooted, and they looked round.

"Excuse me," said Bert Monkey, politely. "Can you tell me which Mr Noah is called Nat?"

"Oh, Nat – let me see, Nat lives over there in that Ark," said one Mr Noah. "Leave your car here, though. It might scare the animals."

NOAH'S ARKS EVERYWHERE! SOME LITTLE, SOME BIG

So little Noddy and Bert left the car and went over to Nat Noah's great wooden Ark. Animals were walking here and there in pairs, as good as gold.

"Good day," said two brown monkeys to Bert Monkey.

"Good day," said two snakes and slithered between Bert's legs and tripped him up. He was very cross.

Noddy laughed and laughed, and that made Bert crosser still.

"Let's get out of the way of these animals," said Bert Monkey. "They've got no manners! Look – is that Mr Nat Noah over there?"

WHAT A PECULIAR THING!

NODDY and Bert went up to the tall wooden man. "Are you Mr Nat Noah?" asked Bert, holding his tail firmly in his pocket in case it tried any tricks with Mr Noah.

"Yes," said Mr Noah. "Do you want to speak to me? Pray come into my Ark."

"No, thank you," said Bert politely, "It must be crowded enough already! I just wanted to ask you about a rubber you found this morning. It belongs to me."

"Does it really?" said Mr Noah, taking a wooden purse out of his pocket. "I'll buy it from you. My son Shem has it, and he likes it."

"Oh no — I don't want to sell it," said Bert. "I've got to give it back to my Grandma."

"Well, go and ask Shem for it then," said Mr Noah. "He's over there. He may want an ice cream or something for it, though."

"Thank you," said Bert, and he and Noddy went over to where a wooden boy was playing with two Ark tigers and lions.

Noddy felt rather scared, because their growls were so loud.

The lions and tigers came sniffing round Bert's ankles. Then his tail came in very useful! It slapped at the animals and scared them away!

"Good day, Shem," said Bert. "I believe you have a rubber of mine that your father found and gave to you."

"Oh, that!" said Shem. "Yes, but I didn't want it. I gave it away for an ice cream."

Bert and Noddy stared at him in dismay. It seemed as if they would never, never catch up with that magic rubber!

"Who did you give it to?" asked Bert Monkey. "Somebody here, I hope."

"Well, no," said Shem. "It was someone from Toy Town who came over here by train to borrow one of our Noah's Ark dogs for a night. He always borrows a dog when he leaves his house empty for a night or two. His name is Mr Tubby Bear."

"Mr Tubby Bear!" said Noddy, amazed. "But good gracious me, he's a bear who lives next door to *me!*"

"Does he?" said Shem. "Well, then, you'll know where to find him. I gave him the rubber for his little boy-bear, Master Tubby Bear."

"Did you *really*," said Noddy. "What a very peculiar thing indeed. To think I've come all the way here, miles and miles – and all the time the rubber is back in Toy Town, just next door to me!"

—❦ 8 ❧—

BACK TO TOY TOWN

"We'd better hurry back," said Bert Monkey. "If Mr Tubby Bear is going away for a night or two, he may be gone before we get there!"

"Yes – quick, let's get back into the car," said little Noddy, his head nodding so fast that Bert could hardly see it. "Oh dear – I do hope Master Tubby Bear doesn't try rubbing anything out with the rubber, because if he finds that it is magic I know that he will be very naughty with it."

"Goodness – you must drive at top speed then," said Bert, worried. "I don't want him to use up all the magic in it. My Grandma would be very cross."

"Here we are," said Noddy, running up to his little car. "Get in. And DO keep your tail out of my way. If it starts hooting the hooter again I'll pull it off and throw it into the road."

"Don't you dare do any such thing!" said Bert Monkey, looking very fierce. "If you do, I'll pull off your hat and throw it into the pond."

Noddy at once took off his hat and sat on it, bell and all. Bert sat on his tail too.

"And just see it stays there," said Noddy, fiercely, putting on his hat again. "Here we go!"

And off they went back to Toy Town again, Noddy's bell jingling loudly.

Would they find the Tubby Bears at home?

They drove at top speed into Toy Town, nearly knocking down the lamp post at the corner. It swayed as they went by but didn't quite topple over. What a good thing!

Noddy pulled up outside Mr Tubby Bear's house. The baker was just going by and Noddy called to him.

"Oh, Mr Crumbs! Was there anyone in when you called at Mr Tubby's?"

"They've just gone away," said Mr Crumbs. "They wanted to hire your car to go to the station, little Noddy, but you weren't in."

Noddy felt as if he would burst into tears! They had missed that magic rubber again!

THE BAKER WAS GOING BY AND NODDY CALLED
TO HIM

"Bother, bother, bother!" said Bert Monkey. "Mr Crumbs, do you know where the Tubbies have gone?"

"No," said the baker. "I don't know at all. They've left a dog in the house, I know, because I heard it barking – rather a wooden kind of bark, so I expect it's a Noah's Ark dog. But where the Tubbies have gone to I really couldn't tell you."

He went on his way, and Noddy and Bert looked at one another gloomily.

"NOW what on earth shall we do?" said Bert Monkey.

MASTER TUBBY BEAR HAS A
GOOD TIME

"LET'S look in at the windows and see if we can spy the rubber anywhere," said Noddy. "I'm sure that if we could see it Mr Tubby wouldn't mind us opening a window and getting inside to fetch it."

"But what about the dog?" said Bert. "He might bite us."

"I'll go into my house and find a bone," said Noddy. "He might like that so much that he wouldn't bother about us. You wait here a minute."

"All right," said Bert.

So Bert Monkey waited while Noddy went to find a bone. He came back in a few minutes with a nice big one.

"Now let's look in at the windows," he said, "and see if we can spy that rubber!"

So they went to the front windows and peeped in. No – no rubber was to be seen.

"Let's look in at the kitchen window," said Noddy. "That's where Master Tubby Bear keeps his toys – in a little cupboard. Sometimes he leaves them out, and we might see the magic rubber with them. Come round to the kitchen."

So they went round to peep in at the kitchen window – and what a shock they got!

Master Tubby Bear was there, all by himself – and what do you think he was doing? He was using that magic rubber – yes, he really was!

"Look!" said Bert. "He's got it – and he's rubbing out all kinds of things with it!"

Master Tubby was having a wonderful time! He had been rubbing holes in the kitchen table, for bits of the table were missing, and he had also rubbed holes in the walls.

"Quick – we must stop him!" cried Noddy, and he banged at the window. "He will end up rubbing away the whole house! Little Tubby, stop using that rubber!"

—⚬ 10 ⚬—

LITTLE TUBBY IS VERY
NAUGHTY

LITTLE Tubby looked up and waved at
Noddy.

"Look what I'm doing," he cried. "I'm having
a lovely time!"

"Wuff-wuff-wuff!" said the little Noah's Ark
dog, running into the kitchen to see what all the
shouting was about.

"My Daddy and Mummy have gone away for
the night and they've got this Noah's Ark dog to
look after me," shouted little Tubby. "Would you
like to come and share this rubber with me?"

"Tubby, open the window and give me the rubber," cried Noddy. "It belongs to Bert Monkey. He's come to fetch it. Give it to him."

"No," said little Tubby. "No, I won't. I like it. It's mine."

"Well, stop using it!" yelled Bert Monkey. "Look what you've done – rubbed away half that table! And look at the holes in the walls. What will your mother say?"

"My Daddy gave it to me," said little Tubby. "He said I could use it, so there!"

"But he didn't KNOW that it was magic!" cried Noddy.

"Oooh – is it magic?" said Tubby, pleased. "I thought there was something funny about it. Ooooh – magic!"

And he rubbed a hole right in the middle of the cushion in the rocking-chair!

"We must get in and take it," said Noddy. "He'll rub the whole place away."

TUBBY RUBBED A HOLE IN THE MIDDLE OF
THE CUSHION

"What about the dog?" asked Bert, looking at the Noah's Ark dog fearfully. "He's barking like anything!"

"Noah's Ark dogs are all bark and no bite," said Noddy. "Anyway, we really must be brave. Come on!"

He opened the window wide and climbed in. The wooden dog rushed at him, barking, but brave little Noddy took no notice. He marched straight over to naughty little Tubby Bear.

"Go away! I'll rub you out!" said little Tubby, and that made Noddy stop in a hurry. Goodness – he did not want to be rubbed out by a magic rubber. Bother Tubby – and why must he be so naughty just now? He was usually such a good little bear!

NODDY GETS THE RUBBER
AT LAST

BERT suddenly remembered the bone that Noddy had fetched and he threw it to the barking dog. At once it forgot about Noddy and ran to the bone. Bert got in at the window and went over to Tubby, looking very fierce.

"Now then," he said, "you give me that rubber or I'll take hold of you and throw you out of the window straight into that prickly bush I see out there!"

"You come near me and I'll rub you out," said naughty Tubby, dancing round Bert holding the rubber out in front of him.

Bert's tail suddenly came out of his pocket and tried to snatch away the rubber.

Little Tubby gave the end of it a rub with the rubber – and goodness me, the tip of the tail disappeared!

"Ow! Oooh!" cried Bert. "You've rubbed out the tip of my tail. Stop, Tubby!"

But Tubby didn't stop. He just went mad with the rubber! He rubbed out a kettle, he rubbed out a clock, he even tried to rub out Noddy's hat, but Noddy whipped it off. Neither he nor Bert dared to go too near that wicked little Tubby!

And then Tubby fell over the little wooden dog, and the rubber shot out of his hand into a dark corner. Noddy was after it at once. Good – he had got it.

"NOW!" he said, walking towards naughty little Tubby. "NOW! What shall I rub out first – your nose or your mouth?"

Tubby squealed and ran up the stairs. The dog went after him, carrying its bone. Tubby slammed his bedroom door and locked it – click!

"Well, we've got the rubber at last," said Noddy. "Thank goodness! I can't think what Mrs Tubby will say when she gets home and sees the holes in the table and the walls and everything!"

"She'll have to go to my Grandma and get a Come-Back spell," said Bert. "Give me the rubber, Noddy."

"No," said Noddy. "I want to use it myself for a few things. There is a shelf I want moved out of my cupboard – but the rubber can rub it away – and I'd like to rub out the stains on my steps. Come and watch me, Bert."

THE END OF THE ADVENTURE

BERT went into Noddy's house with Noddy grumbling. "All the magic will be used up. I shall still be in trouble."

His tail suddenly swept round Noddy and slapped the rubber out of his hand. Bert made a grab at it, but Noddy was there first.

"You keep your tail in your pocket or tied round your waist!" cried Noddy crossly. "I'm *tired* of that tail!"

But in half a minute it had tripped Noddy up and almost made him drop the rubber again. He was very cross!

"Now, you sit down in that chair, and don't you DARE move until I've finished rubbing out what I want to," said Noddy to Bert Monkey – and he really looked so very fierce that Bert sat down in fright.

Bert was tired. His eyes closed. He gave a tiny little snore, and his tail crept out of his pocket and reached out to where Noddy was rubbing out the shelf he didn't need in his cupboard. Its tip slid into Noddy's pocket to see what it could find.

Noddy put his hand into his pocket to get his hanky – and he felt the tail! He held on to it fast – and then, whatever do you think he did?

Yes – you are quite right –he rubbed it out with the magic rubber! He rubbed the whole of it away, right up to where it joined on to Bert Monkey. Aha, Bert Monkey, that will teach you to look after your tail in future!

NODDY RUBBED BERT'S TAIL OUT WITH THE
MAGIC RUBBER

Bert woke up just when Noddy had finished all his rubbing-out jobs. He looked at Noddy's clock and jumped to his feet.

"My goodness – I must take that rubber back to my Grandma this very minute," he said. "Give me the rubber, Noddy, please do!"

Noddy gave it to him with a grin. "Here you are. Thanks for the adventure, Bert Monkey. We've had quite an exciting time today, haven't we?"

"We certainly have," said Bert, and went out to get his bicycle which was still leaning against the wall, just where he had left it this morning.

"Look after that tail of yours!" yelled Noddy, and Bert nodded back to him. "It's all right, Noddy, it's in my pocket!"

But it wasn't. It was rubbed out. Oh Noddy, whatever will Bert say when he knows what you have done to his BEAUTIFUL tail?

Noddy counted out all the money that Bert had given him that morning. What a lot! He could buy a new pot of bright paint for his little car.

"That was a real adventure today," he said to the car when he went to put it away. "Shall we look for another one, little car? I DO like adventures!"

"Parp-parp!" said the car. "So do I, Noddy. Parp-parp!"

Noddy went singing into his little house. Can you hear him?

> *"Oh, what an adventure*
> *We've both had today,*
> *In search of a rubber*
> *That rubs things away —*
> *Poor old Bert Monkey,*
> *How he will stare,*
> *When he looks for his tail*
> *And he can't see it there!*
> *Rubbity-rubbity-rub!*
> *Oh, what an adventure!*
> *I think I will go*
> *And tell it to Big-Ears,*
> *He'll laugh - ho-ho-ho!*
> *Rubbity-rubbity-rub!"*